THE ADVENTURES of

Created and Written by
Calvin T. Mann

Forward by Calvin Mann

This book is about friendship. It started as joke. Friends gathering in the studio; Oba, Tyler, Latrel, Sun Ray, and our music. We were just some men getting together, always laughing, dreaming of making it off our little street on Murray Hill in Detroit, Mi. Within the laughter however, our dear friend Oba was suffering from MS. As his condition progressed, as he was losing the battle, his strength and resolve, some days the only thing he had to hold onto was the laughter. While recording in the studio one day, I announced I was going to create a children's book and title it 'The Adventures of Oba and Luther. That created the biggest laugh of the day, what a silly idea. Weeks later, Tyler asked about the book. I started a dialog of the voices and we laughed until tears flowed from our eyes.

I saw how my children Dominique and Cameron bonded with Oba and were loving of him. One day, and to the disbelief of many, I began to write this story, the first of what I hope to be many. I wanted to be that role model to my children, grandchildren and those that come after I am gone. One they could admire, critique and/or appreciate, but to know a little bit more about me being a man of purpose and my commitment to my word, to family and friends and the community I support.
A few years later, Oba passed away. The day of the funeral I held up my phone to Latrel and showed him the book cover, He smiled. I showed Tyler. He smiled. With my good bye to Oba, and in honor of his friendship, I finished the book.

This book is about building true friendships. It doesn't matter what you are, your age or your color, what matters is connecting with others, and if you are lucky enough like I have been, you will create friendships that last a lifetime. And when they are gone, a piece of them will always be with you.
A loving shout out to my family! 'Live your greatest dream' and thank you for being mine. To all of you, this is only the beginning in this series that will serve as an inspiration to all those that read, to continue my mission to support others, as I have done for over 34 years. Remember, 'Love is the One Thing You Can Take to Heaven".

Encourage Me! I'm Young!

"DEDICATION"

DEDICATION by Calvin T. Mann

This book is dedicated to the children of the world

who follow, but in reality, truly lead. God has the last

word, so"live your greatest dreams" and know

"I am Possible

To my CHILDREN GO FOR YOUR DREAMS DAD LOVES YOU !

Young Luther is curious about where he and his family are moving. He asks, "Dad, do you think I'll meet some friends my age?" His father, Mr. Cunningham, responds, "Luther, I am sure you will meet all kinds of people here.

"There are some great schools here, like BelCol Middle School. Luther, I'm so excited for you!" " Thanks Dad," Luther replied. The movers are still taking stuff into the house as they pull into the driveway.

They shake hands. As the movers are just about done, the Jenkins family head home. Then Luther turns to Oba and says, "Hey Oba, what's it like here?"

Oba answers, "It's very interesting!"
Every day I get to go on an adventure.
Of course, my parents don't know, but
Abu makes sure that I always
come home.

Luther says, "Abu... who's
Abu?" "Oh you will see,"
replies Oba. Suddenly, Mrs. Cunningham
calls Luther and he takes off yelling,
"see you tomorrow Oba!"

The next day Oba is standing in front of his home playing with his baseball and glove, throwing the ball in the air. "Hey Oba," says Luther.
Oba replies, "Good morning Luther, how did you sleep last night?"

Luther answers, "what an amazing night!, I slept very well but I kept dreaming about your friend Abu. What does he look like?"
"He's just an old wise mole that helps me. Hey, can you ask your parents if you can go to the field to play baseball with me?" asked Oba.

Luther runs home and asks, "mom, dad, can i go with our new neighbor Oba to the park to play ball? It's right up the street."

They both said yes. As he leaves, mom says, "your father said be careful!"

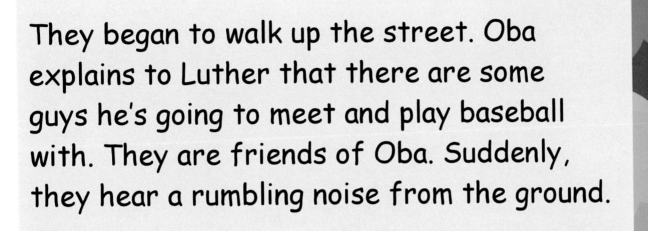

They began to walk up the street. Oba explains to Luther that there are some guys he's going to meet and play baseball with. They are friends of Oba. Suddenly, they hear a rumbling noise from the ground.

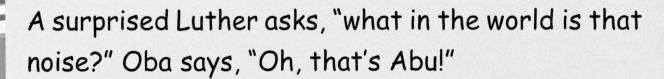

A surprised Luther asks, "what in the world is that noise?" Oba says, "Oh, that's Abu!"

Out of the ground comes Abu, the wise mole who wears an African cap known as a Kofi. Abu exclaims, "Well hello Oba! What might our adventure be today?"

Abu whispers, "Listen. If you go to your right, there are some kids who are in the same age group, however, they may be just a little rowdy.

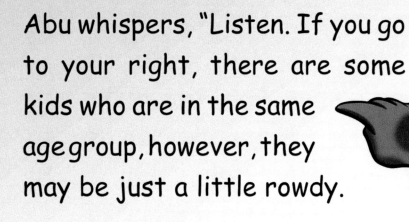

But, he chuckles, if you go left, everyone is in the same grade as Oba. Luther would be the youngest, but he will be accepted."

14

Luther asks Oba, "Which way do you choose?" Oba thinks a moment and asks Luther, "Which way do you think is best?" They decide after talking together.

Oba tells Abu, "we want to go left." Just then, the road opens to them and Abu says, "proceed, young men! Enjoy your decision. Remember, you can do anything you want! Live your greatest dream!"

As Oba and Luther leave, Abu disappears just as quickly as he arrived.

Oba and Luther arrived at the park. No one was there yet so they began to play catch, "Nice catch Luther," said Oba. "Thank you," said Luther. "Hey, try to catch this one Luther," said Oba.
As the ball began to come down, a group of kids ran over yelling, "hey Oba!"

18

The group of kids asked, "who's your friend Oba?"
"This is Luther. Let's go play some ball!" Oba said.

The game begins. The guy on first base yells out, "Hey, how old is Luther?" Oba replies, "He's nine." "Okay," the first baseman says, "Let's go!"

20

Luther wants to watch before getting involved in the game. Oba walks over to him and says, "Come on. They want you to play, and we'll help you with whatever you need to know."

Luther will be short stop when they get on the field because Oba thinks he has a strong arm.

The game begins, and Luther asks if he can bat first. His teammates tell him he has to work hard if he is going to be up first.

Oba agrees and Luther is first to the plate.

Oba doesn't know it, but Luther's uncle taught him how to bat pretty well. The first was a strike. Luther's teammates said to him, "it's okay young guy." On the second pitch, Luther swings and "Whack!" The ball is hit deep and it's a double!"

Oba chuckles as he walks to the plate. He looks at the faces of the other team because they didn't think Luther had a chance.

Oba is smiling, waiting on the right pitch. He hits the ball and it's a double, bringing Luther home. Oba yells out, "Nice job Luther!" Luther replies, "You too! We're up one to nothing!"

25

The game continues and Oba as well as Luther were having a great time.

Luther gets a hit and headed for second base; then turning for third base.

He is tripped by the shortstop who says, "whoops!" Luther falls and has to go back to second base.

BALL   STRIKE   OUT

VISI   2 3 4 5 6 7 8 9 10

Oba yells to Luther, "are you ok? Yes, i'm fine," says Luther with a determined voice. They play on and Oba and Luther's team is winning the game 3-2. Then the other team takes the lead on a long shot in the corner. The score is now 4-3, last inning!

As they are exchanging the field, Oba approaches
the short stop and stops the entire game. He
says, "Before we finish this game, I think you owe
Luther an apology for tripping him." The short
stop says, "I don't owe him anything! He is younger
than all of us and shouldn't be playing."

Oba, being the team leader, calls Luther over and asks, "Luther, do you think he tripped you on purpose? If so, would you apologize if it were you?" Luther thought about how his parents always taught him to be honest. He can see his mom saying, "Luther always tell the truth, because lying only makes things worse." Luther then answers "yes, I would apologize. I honestly thought he did it on purpose. I'm not hurt though."

Oba asks the shortstop, "were you trying to bully Luther? Maybe intimidate him? Can you be honest like Luther?"

Everyone is watching. The shortstop looks around and says, "I'm sorry Luther. You were better than I thought, so I tried to trip you up. Will you forgive me?'

Luther shook hands with the Shortstop and the game goes on.

It's getting late in the day, right around dinner time and the game is a good one. It's two outs, and as usual, up to bat is Oba. Luther is on base. In all the years Oba has played baseball, he has never done well in this situation. He flashed back to when he played for the BelCol Middle School's team in the Spring. They were up for the championship and he struck out. Oba gets up to bat and Luther shouts, "Oba, you're about to make this the greatest day for me! I've never won a game like this!" Oba chokes up. His first swing is a strike Luther yells, "I believe in you!" Now, Oba focuses and hits a triple. Bringing home Luther Oba gets a walk off the triple.

The teams met in the middle jumping up and down. "Great game guys!" says Oba. Suddenly, Oba hears his dad call out, " Oba Jenkins, time to come home!" Oba and Luther started walking away. The field clears and suddenly they are back on the block walking home.

Oba says, "Luther, how did you like our adventure today?" Luther said, "What a day Oba. We had a great time as friends. That was awesome!"

"Oba, I hope you will be my friend. My parents like you, and I do too." Oba smiles and says, "Thank you Luther, I like you too. See you tomorrow."

Oba gets home and he is excited to tell his father about the entire day. "Dad, Luther can really play baseball! We won the Game! He played well for a young guy."

Dad chuckles, "did you learn any lessons today?" Oba says, "yes, I sure did. One of the guys tripped Luther. I stopped the game to say something when the time was right. Then, Luther told the truth that he was tripped by the shortstop. Being a friend is about honesty and support, right dad?"

Dad answered, "yes son."

"The shortstop admitted and apologized for trying to trip Luther. It was just before the last inning." Dad smiled and said, "Good job son. Always being a leader." Oba interrupts, "but wait dad, I have to tell how Luther helped me. Remember, I have never hit a ball that won a game until today! Luther said that he believed in me. On the second pitch, I hit a walk off triple to bring him home! It was so exciting! We jumped up and down, that's when I heard you call us home." Oba's dad said, "Oba, there's nothing you can't do! You can always live your greatest dream." Oba thinks to himself about Abu. He always says that to him too. He then stares out the window. Luther is doing the same thing.

Luther turns to his parents and says, "mom, dad, I believed in Oba today and he didn't let me down. I think I have found a best friend in Oba Jenkins." Mr. Cunningham, Luther's dad says, "Luther, you were honest today and a good friend to Oba. I am proud of you." "Thanks dad, I was proud also." Luther chuckles as he thinks about Abu. Dad asked, "What's funny Luther?"

Luther starts to tell him but decided to just say, "I am glad we moved here. Thanks mom and dad."

The day closes with
both families at their
dinner tables,

talking and enjoying
each other's company.

Man cannot stand
alone in his victory.

THE END

"Live Your Greatest Dream"

Made in the USA
Monee, IL
03 September 2021